Donated to

Timothy Christian School

in honor of

Dominic DiLeo

on

May 14, 1998

Birthday Book Club

Presented to

_____

from

_____

_____

_____ *19* ____

The King's Alphabet

A Bible Book about Letters

The King's Alphabet

Copyright 1988, 1989 by Word Publishing.

ISBN 0-8499-0713-6 (formerly ISBN 0-8344-0162-2)

Library of Congress Cataloging-in-Publication Data

Hollingsworth, Mary, 1947-
    The King's Alphabet : a Bible book about letters / concept by Cheryl Rico and Ginger Knight ; illustrated by Mary Grace Eubank ; text by Mary Hollingsworth.
        p.   cm.
    Reprint. Originally published: Fort Worth, Tex. : Worthy Pub., ©1988.
    Summary: Through whimsical rhymes and animal antics, children discover both the alphabet and God's creations.
    ISBN 0-8499-0713-6
    [1. Christian life — Fiction. 2. Animals — Fiction. 3. Stories in rhyme. 4. Alphabet.] I. Rico, Cheryl, 1951-   . II. Knight, Ginger, 1954-   . III. Eubank, Mary Grace, ill. IV. Title.
PZ8.3.H7196Ki   1989
[E] — dc20   89-78145
                                                                        CIP
                                                                         AC

Printed in the United States of America.

012349LB9876543

The King's Alphabet

A Bible Book about Letters

Concept by: Cheryl Rico and Ginger Knight
Illustrated by: Mary Grace Eubank
Text by: Mary Hollingsworth

WORD
Kids!

WORD PUBLISHING
Dallas · London · Vancouver · Melbourne

Dear Parents,

The alphabet. It's the basis of all reading. It's one of the most important tools of education you can share with your child. And with **The King's Alphabet** your child will learn, laugh and love God all at the same time.

The King's Alphabet is a delightful combination of poetry and colorful, happy art by one of the world-famous Sesame Street artists. It's filled with gentle reminders that God created everything in our world.

Like Dr. Seuss, Mother Goose and other classic teaching books, the amusing poems and entertaining animals help your child *enjoy* learning the alphabet. And that enjoyment will bring your child back to **The King's Alphabet** over and over again.

Repeating the sound of the alphabet letter on each page is a fun and effective way of teaching children the unique sounds of each letter. As you read aloud, help your child find the many items on the page whose names begin with that sound. Encourage the child to say the words along with you, and the alphabet will soon become a familiar tool to unlock God's wonderful world.

Settle down now with your child and **The King's Alphabet** for a time of fun and learning about everything from angelfish to zebras . . . and the God of love who created them all. It's a repeatable experience!

The Publisher

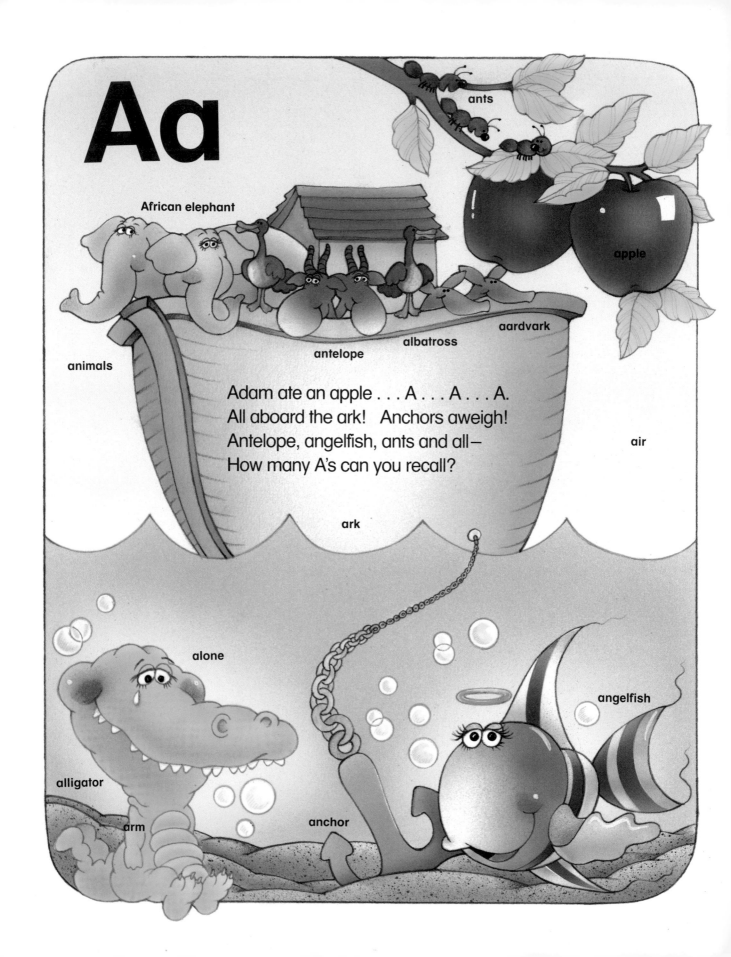

Aa

ants

African elephant

apple

aardvark

albatross

antelope

animals

Adam ate an apple . . . A . . . A . . . A.
All aboard the ark!   Anchors aweigh!
Antelope, angelfish, ants and all—
How many A's can you recall?

air

ark

alone

angelfish

alligator

arm

anchor

Bb

balloons

bell

bluebird

B is as easy as it can be.
Butterflies, bluebirds and
bumblebees.
Blueberries, buttercups, bugs
eating bread.
We read the Bible to know
what God said.

butterfly

bark

bear

bumblebees

Bible

bow

book

buttercups

brown bag

basketball

bread

buttons

blueberries

bottle

bugs

banana

butter

Cc

cheek

child

chocolate
chip cookie

coat of
many colors

camel

chin

colt

carrot

chew

cape

C is simple, can't you see?
Camels and colts carry cargo
for free.
A cheetah is chasing a calico cat,
And Joseph's new coat needs a
matching sun hat.

chicken

can

cheetah

canary

caterpillar

calico cat

chase

Dd

A, B, C and then comes D.
Dolphins dive down into God's deep sea.
Daffodils, donkeys, Dalmatians—what luck!
Here comes a mama and five downy ducks.

Ee

eye

eagle

ear

elephant

elk

elbow

E is as easy as C and D.
Eagles fly high with the greatest
of ease.
Elephants, elks, emus and eels.
Earthworms are wiggly and icky
to feel.

eaglet

emu

envelope

eight eggs

earth

earthworm

Hey, look! Hey, look! H is here.
Happy hyenas and halibuts cheer.
Hippos and hamsters, hound dogs and hawks.
Have you ever seen how a hedgehog walks?

Ii

I see you, but where am I?
I am in insects, inchworm
and isle.
Ivy is itchy, an iris is shy.
God made iguanas, but I
wonder why.

ice cream

iris

insects

iguana

island

inchworm

ivy

jumprope

Jj

jaguar

jungle

juniper

jackrabbit

jonquils

E, F, G, H, I and J.
Jellyfish jiggle as they swim away.
Do jackrabbits jump over juniper shrubs
Or jaguars munch on jonquil bulbs?

jasmine

jack-in-the-box

jelly beans

jellyfish

Jonah

Kk

kite

key

K follows J, and that's okay.
Jesus says, "Be kind today."
Hide-n-seek's fun for a
kangaroo's kid.
Can you climb a tree like
the katydid?

koala

kangaroo

kick

katydid

kittens

Ll

light

lion

love

lamb

land

lilies

llama

Well, well, well, next comes L.
Lilies, lions and leopards—do tell!
Moonlight and sunlight; lost
lambs and Levites.
Lick a big lemon, but don't take
a bite!

lick

lemon

leopard

leg

Levite

Mm

mountain

moose

mango

monkey

munch

mane

M . . . M . . . M . . .
marvelous M!
Monkeys munch mangoes and
swing limb to limb.
A moose and a mule don't moo
or bray.
And what, I wonder, does a
mantis pray?

mirror

mouth

praying mantis

mail

mittens

muskrat

mouse

milk

mushrooms

mule

Nn

nest

night

neck

Noah

Noah's boat

nose

newt

nutshell

numbers

nine

N is next. Now please take note . . .
God sent the animals to Noah's boat:
Long-necked giraffes and hook-nosed birds —
All God's best from flocks and herds.

Oo

owl

opossum

orange

olive tree

octopus

otter

ostrich

oatmeal

ocean

Oh, oh, oh! Did you know
That O is a wonderful letter
to know?
Octopus, ostrich and
olive trees.
Love one another, and obey
God, please.

Pp

P is perfect to follow O.
Plop, plop, plop is how ponies go.
God gives pandas and pigs
        tasty treats,
But a porcupine's hug is not
        very sweet.

peach

pony

pond

penguin

pig

parakeet

panda

Popsicle

pie

peanut
butter

pear

pickle

pumpkin

pineapple

plum

potato

peas

pajamas

polka dot

pansies   porcupine

Qq

L, M, N, O, P and Q.
Queens ask questions, like
"How do you do?"
Jonathan used a quiver
of arrows.
And God sent quail, but why
not sparrows?

Rr

rainbow

rays

R . . . R . . . R . . . We've come this far.
Robins and ravens both start with R.
Rhinos are rare, rabbits are hares.
Rainbows are God's way of
showing He cares.

road

roof

river

robin

ribbon

rabbit

rose

ring-'round-the-rosy

raccoon

rhinoceros

rat

red radio

rock

Ss

snake

stork

sun

S is so simple and easy to say.
Samson was strong; so, he saved the day.
God sends the sunshine and showers we need.
Can you snare a seahorse with ropes of seaweed?

seagulls

sandwich

seal

sailboat

Samson

sand

shark

snorkel

spider

squid

sea

seaweed

seahorse

scissors

starfish

shell

snail

Toot, toot, toot! Make way for T.
Thank you, God, for tall, tall trees.
Turtles are tardy; turkeys eat grain.
Can you teach a tuna to ride in
a train?

Uu

Q, R, S, T . . . where are U?
Hiding inside an urn of blue?
Does a monkey's uncle live up in
a tree?
God made the universe for you
and me.

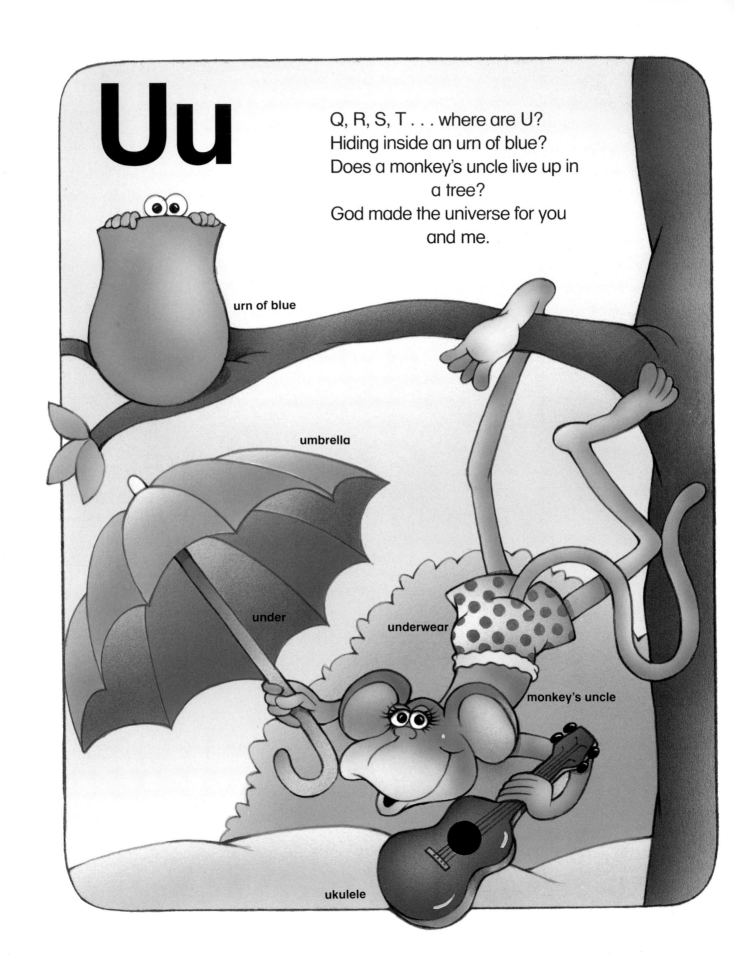

urn of blue

umbrella

under

underwear

monkey's uncle

ukulele

violets

vase

vine

vulture

Vv

voyage

V is in village and voyage and veil.
You can say A up to V very well.
Violets and vultures and
          vegetable vines.
To whom do vipers send
          valentines?

viper

violin

village

veil

valentine

SHOP

SCHOOL

Ww

Pardon me, I hate to trouble you,
But where would I look to find W?
In walrus and wasp and weasel,
you say?
Do woodpeckers get headaches
from pecking all day?

Xx Yy Zz

At last we come to X, Y, Z.
Exotic birds and yellow bees.
Zithers and zebras; before
you forget,
Can you now repeat the King's
Alphabet?

Books for Children

Children of the King Series:

The King's Alphabet
    A Bible Book about Letters

The King's Numbers
    A Bible Book about Counting

Young Friends Series:

I'm No Ordinary Chicken
Nobody Likes Me
Will You Be My Friend?

Bible Books:

International Children's Bible
Read-n-Grow Picture Bible
What Does God Do?
Amy Grant's Heart-to-Heart Bible Stories